To Ava—Nothing is better than you!

THE MUSEUM OF NOTHING

STEVEN GUARNACCIA

Oona and Otto are going to
the museum. They want to visit
one they've never been to before.

They've been to the Museum of Very Large Paintings

and the Museum of Very Important Inventions.

They come to a street they've
never seen before.

At the end of the street is a
large door that says . . .

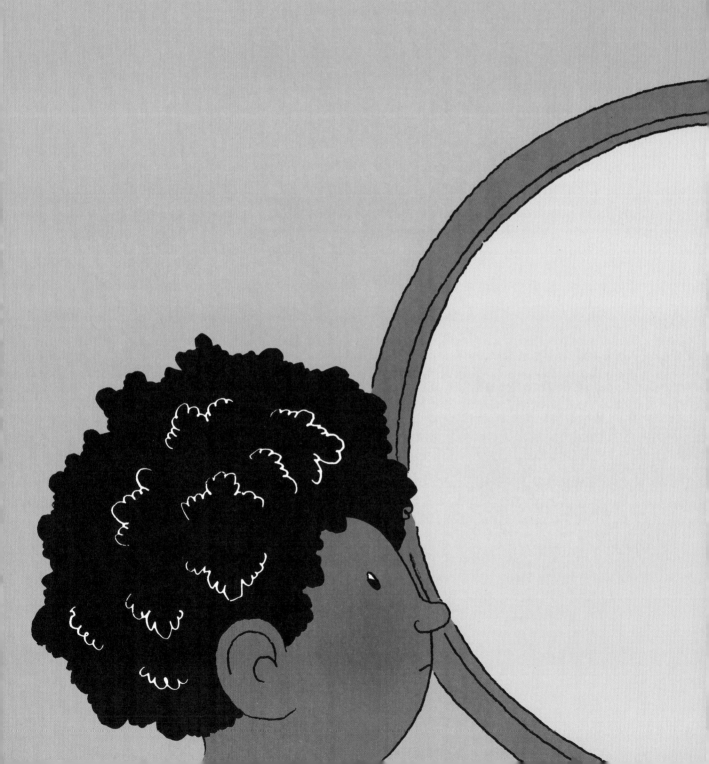

They step inside.

The museum is filled with . . .

. . . nothing.

NOTHING
THROUGH HERE

There is nothing
everywhere.

NOTHING
THIS WAY

THE **BUPKIS** GALLERY

There is nothing in the sculpture gallery.

THE POPPED BUBBLE

BUST of the UNKNOWN SOLDIER

OUT TO LUNCH

And nothing in the bottles of air from around the world.

And there's nothing in the Nobody Room.

The Man Who Wasn't There

As I was going

Up the stair

I met a man

Who wasn't there.

He wasn't there

Again today,

Oh, how I wish

He'd go

Away.

In the Blank Library,
all the books have
empty pages.

Each is about a different kind of nothing.

In the Zero Wing, they see the world's most beautiful nothings.

HOLE IN THE WALL

MOUSE HOLE

BUTTON HOLES

SWISS CHEESE HOLES

Then they visit the Hall of Holes.

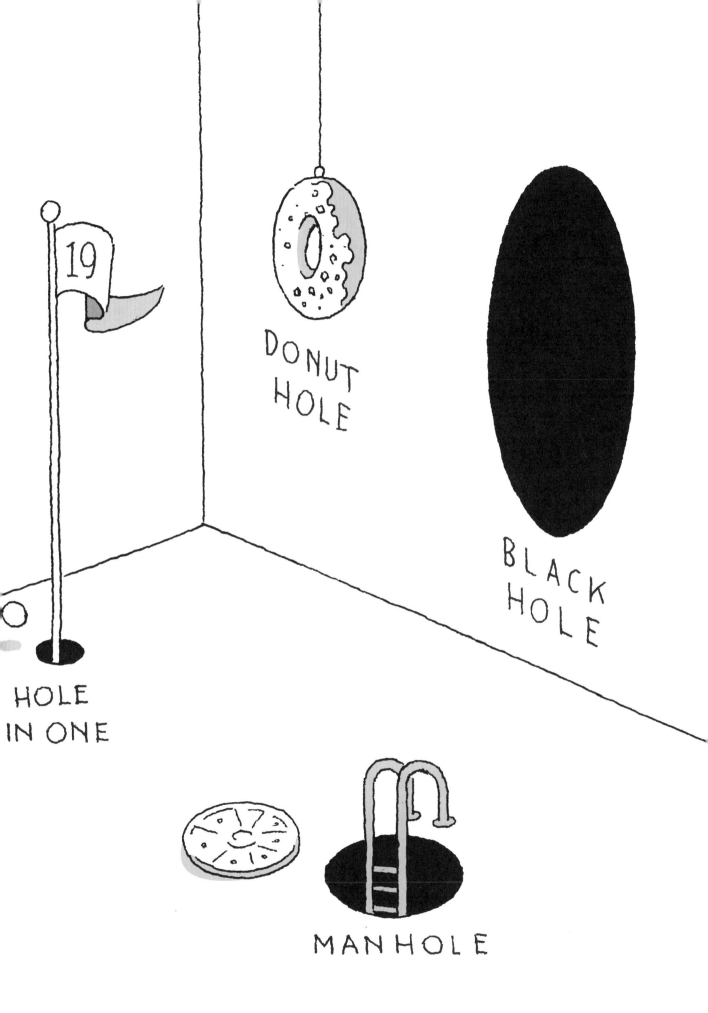

19

DONUT
HOLE

BLACK
HOLE

HOLE
IN ONE

MANHOLE

Otto gets too close to the Black Hole
and is suddenly sucked into it.

BLACK
HOLE

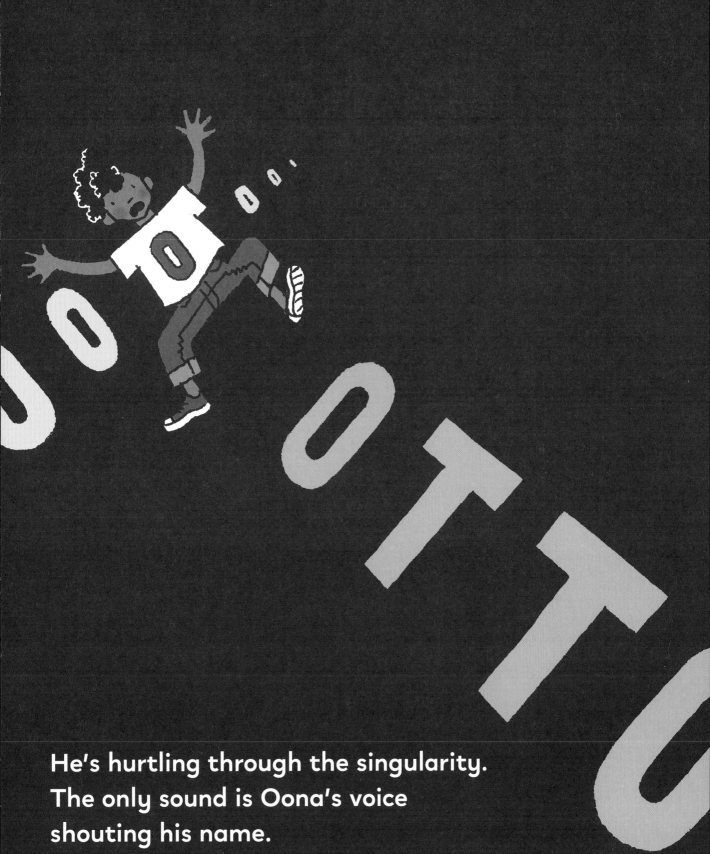

He's hurtling through the singularity.
The only sound is Oona's voice
shouting his name.

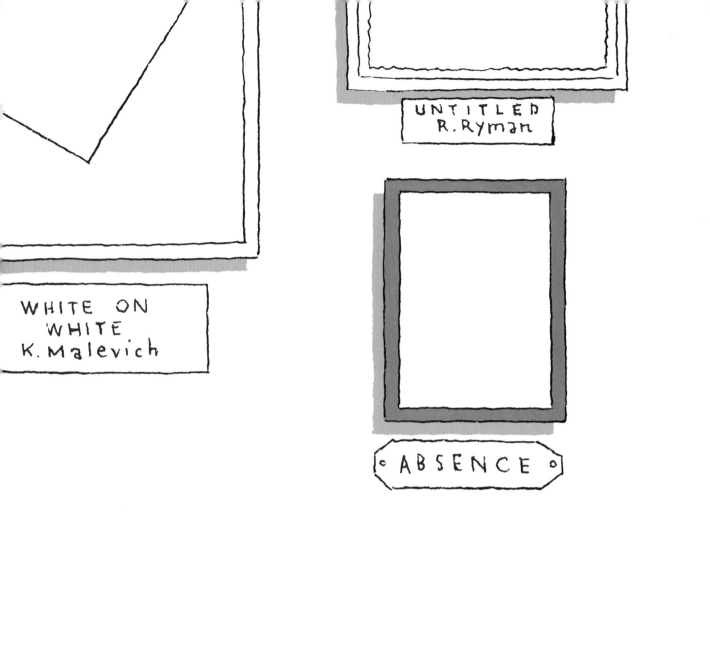

UNTITLED
R. Ryman

WHITE ON
WHITE
K. Malevich

◦ ABSENCE ◦

Oona looks for Otto everywhere.

POLAR BEAR IN
A SNOWSTORM

ERASED
DE KOONING
DRAWING
R. Rauschenberg

Lost at the Museum
M.T. WALLS

BUY NOTHING
GHOST CARDS
THE MUSEUM
BOX of NOTHING
NOW! WITH 0% MORE NOTHING !!!!

Before leaving, Oona and Otto shop for souvenirs.

Outside the museum, they turn around for one last look.

There is nothing there.

THE CATALOG OF
THE MUSEUM OF NOTHING

Here's **"nothing"** in some other languages:

Arabic: شَيْ · لَا (la shi)
Chinese: 没有 (Méiyǒu)
French: Rien
German: Nichts
Italian: Niente
Spanish: Nada
Swahili: Hakuna kitu

Isamu Noguchi was a Japanese American artist who lived from 1904 to 1988 and created iconic sculptures, public art, and furniture designs with flowing, organic shapes that often incorporated empty space.

Bupkis is a Jewish American word for "nothing" that evolved from the Yiddish word "bobkes," meaning "nonsense" or "nothing."

The Tomb of the Unknown Soldier in Virginia's Arlington National Cemetery is a monument dedicated to all those killed in war whose remains have not been found or identified.

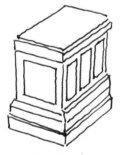

UNKNOWN
SOLDIER

The French artist Marcel Duchamp, who made art he called "readymades" by choosing simple everyday objects and declaring them works of art, bought an empty glass cannister in 1919 and named it **50 cc of Paris Air**. Today it is on display at the Philadelphia Museum of Art.

The Invisible Man is a science fiction novel by the British writer H. G. Wells, published in 1897, in which a scientist named Griffin discovers a way to make the human body more like air, so that it neither absorbs nor reflects light. He tries it out on himself and becomes invisible.

A novel called **Invisible Man**, by the American writer Ralph Ellison, was published in 1952. It is narrated by a Black man, whose name we never learn, who reflects on his lifetime of confronting the social invisibility that racism creates in the U.S.

The innovative American poet Emily Dickinson's poem **"I'm Nobody! Who Are You?"** was not published until 1891, five years after her death.

The rhyming verse **"I Met a Man Who Wasn't There"** has been adapted many times over many years from a poem written by the American poet Hughes Mearns in 1899, inspired by reports of a ghost that haunted a house in Nova Scotia, Canada.

Dr. No, a 1957 spy novel by the British writer Ian Fleming, became the first film in the James Bond series in 1962. *Dr. No* is also the title of a 2022 novel by Percival Everett about a professor of mathematics who is an expert on nothing.

Zilch is a slang term for "nothing" or "zero" that became popular in the twentieth century. No one is certain where "zilch" came from.

In his book ***Being and Nothingness***, published in 1943, the French philosopher Jean-Paul Sartre found that "nothingness"—for example, the absence of a friend—is always something real and concrete.

Much Ado About Nothing is a comedy written in 1598–1599 by the great British playwright William Shakespeare, in which several funny misunderstandings or "nothings" get in the way of romantic love.

In the 1939 mystery novel ***And Then There Were None***, by the British writer Agatha Christie, eight guests are invited to an island by an unknown host, and one by one, they are all found dead.

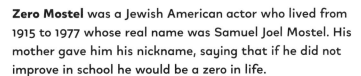

Zero Mostel was a Jewish American actor who lived from 1915 to 1977 whose real name was Samuel Joel Mostel. His mother gave him his nickname, saying that if he did not improve in school he would be a zero in life.

HOLE
IN WALL

A **hole in the wall** is an expression meaning a very basic, small, unfancy restaurant.

A **black hole** is a place in space that no one can see, because gravity is so strong that even light cannot get out.

OTTO?

BLACK
HOLE

A **singularity** means a point where something is infinite. The singularity at the center of a black hole is a place where matter is so compressed, to such an infinitely small point, that it doesn't really exist anymore.

The Russian artist Kazimir Malevich's 1918 painting *White on White* shows a white square on a canvas painted white, with just a tiny bit of contrast between the two whites.

Robert Ryman was an American painter who lived from 1930 to 2019 and made many untitled paintings that appeared to be shades of white against other shades of white.

The American artist Robert Rauschenberg's famous work *Erased de Kooning Drawing* is a nearly blank piece of paper in a gold frame, which Rauschenberg made in 1953 by erasing a drawing by fellow artist Willem de Kooning.

THIS PAGE LEFT
INTENTIONALLY
BLANK

An imprint of Astra Books for Young Readers,
a division of Astra Publishing House
astrapublishinghouse.com
Printed in China

ISBN: 978-1-6626-5144-1 (hc)
ISBN: 978-1-6626-5145-8 (eBook)
Library of Congress Control Number: 2022946880

First edition
10 9 8 7 6 5 4 3 2 1

Design by Amelia Mack
The text is set in Quinoa Bold.
The title is handlettered by Steven Guarnaccia.
The illustrations are done in ink and colored digitally.

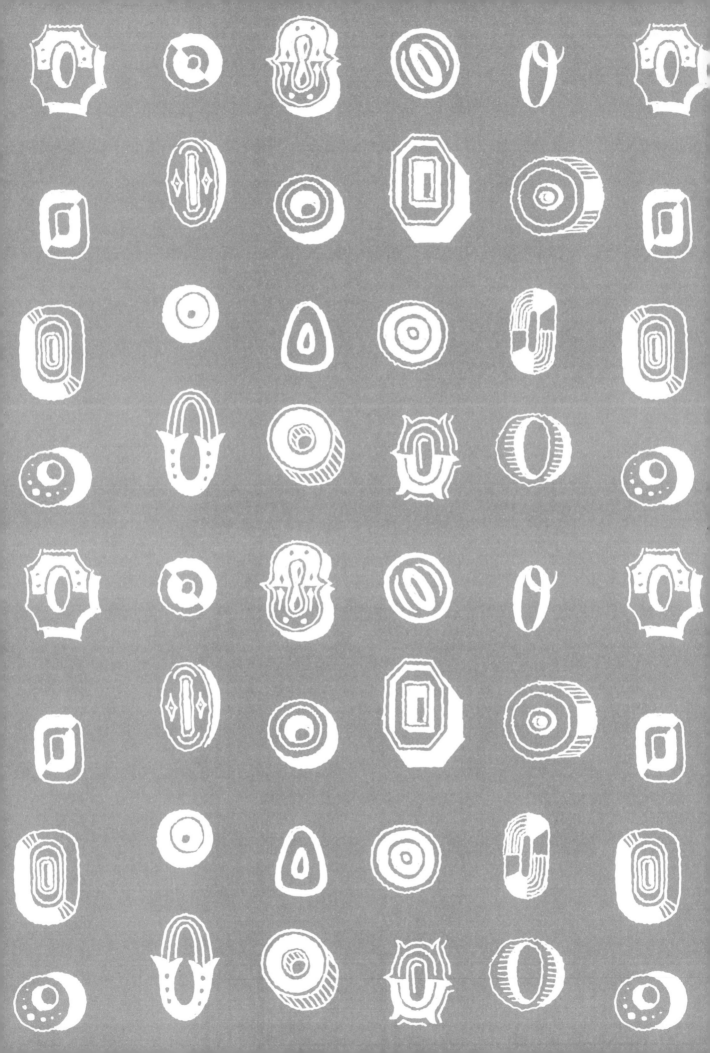